THE GIFT OF ANGER

Suresh Thadhani

INDIA • SINGAPORE • MALAYSIA

Copyright © Suresh Thadhani 2025
All Rights Reserved.

ISBN
Paperback 979-8-89777-498-2
Hardcase 979-8-89777-499-9

This book has been published with all efforts taken to make the material error-free after the consent of the author. However, the author and the publisher do not assume and hereby disclaim any liability to any party for any loss, damage, or disruption caused by errors or omissions, whether such errors or omissions result from negligence, accident, or any other cause.

While every effort has been made to avoid any mistake or omission, this publication is being sold on the condition and understanding that neither the author nor the publishers or printers would be liable in any manner to any person by reason of any mistake or omission in this publication or for any action taken or omitted to be taken or advice rendered or accepted on the basis of this work. For any defect in printing or binding the publishers will be liable only to replace the defective copy by another copy of this work then available.

CONTENTS

About the Author

Suresh Thadhani

The Author is a matured person who is based in Dubai, for the past four and a half decades. He is originally from Bombay (now Mumbai), India. Writing is his forte and he has done quite a few stints in college magazines and social clubs. He has visited many countries, on the six continents, and loves travelling. Many of his stories are based on real time episodes and he churns them out interestingly in a witty way, easy to understand and bringing a smile on readers' lips. In his own words, he says, if I cannot make you laugh in the first five minutes, then I will cry! Interestingly he adds, and as you are a good person, you don't' want me to cry! So, there you go smiling. His core career is based in the accounting field, but he says he wants to be in the field and so has quit accounting!

He believes all of us on this Good Planet are Students of Life, and likewise we too need to be Good in Life too!

DEDICATIONS: My sincere dedications to my loyal family, without their help and support even a shadow of this book would not be a look for the reader!

ACKNOWLEDGEMENTS: My grateful acknowledgements to Publishers and their Team for turning my manuscripts into full-fledged books.

HAPPY READING!

STAY SAFE HEALTHY AND BLESSED.

Dedications and Acknowledgements

I DEDICATE THIS BOOK TO MY LOYAL FAMILY. WITHOUT THEIR HELP AND SUPPORT, EVEN A SHADOW OF THIS BOOK WOULD NOT BE VISIBLE TO THE READERS.

CHARACTERS IN THE STORY

ROBIN MARKS: CENTRAL CHARACATER – LEAD PLAYER

MRS. MARK (FONDLY KNOWN AS MOM) ROBIN'S MOTHER

HENRY PHIL: BUSINESSMAN & OWNER OF MARGOA ENTERPRISES FZE, HAVING OFFICES IN DUBAI, ABU DHABI, SAUDI ARABIA, AND JAPAN

EMPLOYEES OF MARGOA ENTERPRISES: ROSY ROSHAN: SECRETARY TO HENRY PHIL

TIM SANDERS - ACCOUNTANT, SANTOSH PILLAI - PRO

SALES TEAM: CATHERINE TOLEDA – SALES MANAGER, TONY MIRANDA, LOBO FERANDES, JOSE PHILIPS, JASMINE KAUR SALES STAFF

ANGELA: GIRL FRIEND OF ROBIN

MS BHARATI: FREE LANCE YOGA TEACHER

HARILAL KARAMCHAND: OWNER OF PARADISE IMPORT AND EXPORT LTD. DUBAI,

A VERY SUCCESSFUL BUSINESS HOUSE OPERATING SINCE 1970, HAVING EMPLOYEES:

SHEELA DASWANI: SECRETARY TO HARILAL KARAMCHAND

KRISHNA PILLAI (ACCOUNTANT), SHRIKANT SHINDE (PRO AND LEGAL ADVISOR)

RAMU (HELPER)

SALES STAFF: SUNDER, RAJU, JOSEPH, LEENA, DAVID, RANJEET

1. The Interview

glanced at my watch: 2.40pm. Right time, I was still ahead by 20 minutes for the interview.

MERRY PLAZA was just in front of me – a mere crossing of the road and I would be stepping in the boulevard. Inside the building, the huge board spelt out the various offices and I could see the office I had to go MARGO ENTERPRISES FZE, ON 2ND Floor. Satisfied with finding the right place at the right time made be a bit easy, but there was a catch: the lift que was longer, and I guessed I could reach the office quicker, were I to climb the stairs !

With quick steps I walked towards the brightly lit up staircase and paced upwards. Ah! There was a mezzanine floor, two staircases up, which added to six stairs up the office. Anyway, I was quite strong enough at 30 years of age and climbing up was not an issue.

I knocked at the door of office 206, and automatically the door slowly oozed inwards, allowing me face the receptionist: a tough looking lady in her early forties, I guessed. She gave me a broad smile and asked my name. I replied "Robin Marks", and she asked me to sit on the adjoining Sofa. She looked at her watch, and wavering her hand leftwards told me to be seated in the next room. I did as I was told, and saw a few men and ladies already seated— perhaps for the interview.

Within a couple of minutes, a dark-skinned lady walked in with a tray full of half sized water bottles and quickly disappeared the way she came in —- silently and swiftly. Two young men, who were earlier than I, sprang to collect the water bottles, and so did the only lady who was also seated at an arm's length from the men. I was half in mind to take the water bottle. But as I had climbed the stairs and wanted to feel fresh, I took a few sips of water. Then my name was called on the inbuilt speaker in the room. I quickly drank one more sip of water and moved towards the cabin on the right side of the door. In big bold script the name plate read "H E N R Y P H I L MD".

A charming young handsome man was occupying the rich leather and velvet chair. He got up shook my hand, and said "My name is Henry Phil ", and politely pointed to a glass of water for me to take it. "Sir, my name is Robin…. he interrupted. "It is Okay, I have your CV on hand, he cut me short, and asked me to sit down on the opposite sofa facing him. The room was quite cold & I supposed the air conditioner was on full blast.

While he investigated my CV, I casually glanced around the room and found a camera in the corner of his room, as if directly staring at me. That means Henry had watched me all along. Bosses always have a hidden eye, I thought.

So, Robin, you mention you are an all-rounder: in Accounts and Finance, with nine years' experience. And have a driving license too. "Yes Sir" I replied. "No "Sir" Sir" again Henry intervened, just call me by my name: "Henry", he said. I was quite and concentrated on what he was saying.

"If you have finished your water" Let us, go, Henry said, handing me car keys. You drive around the Al Maktoum Street, for the time being, you be the chauffer." I was a bit taken back, but Henry was cheerful, and when he stood in his tall frame of 6 feet 3 inches, he typically looked like a BOSS, every inch of it—personality wise and tone wise. He led me through the back door of his cabin, and soon we were near the elevators. Henry pressed "B" in the elevator, and soon we were in the basement of the building. Opening the door of the lift, some shabby lights greeted us in the basement corridor and Henry told me to press the Ignition Key of his car, so I could spot where the car was. I felt a mixture of joy and fear in my mind and prayed to Almighty I could drive on the busy Al Maktoum Street of Diera, a very busy street always. A grey Camry car started winking. "That is the one, you are going to drive" Henry said. I was thrilled as Angela's car was also Camry' and I was quite used to the dashboard of Camry. My uneasiness gone, I walked to the driver's door and opened the car door. Used to make a walk-around-the car before starting, I slowly moved in a circular way, inspecting the car and while coming to the right side of the door, I gently opened slightly the car door for Henry to sit. He seemed to be pleased with my action and waved his hand. At least, I was now gaining more confidence.

The Car Exit was blinking with green lights, and I had just to take the first right to exit. Carefully, I switched on the ignition lights and noticed Mother Mary's small ivory statue on the car dashboard. I made a sign of the Cross, touched my fingers to my lips and engaged gear and reversed taking care to carefully maneuver the narrow parking lot. Soon I reached the exit point showing a big bright red light ahead of me, which gave me a good glimpse of the right turn I was supposed to make. Getting the clearance, I slowly, looked to the right, and mounted on the road seamlessly. Luckily, this was a Silence Zone area, and there were no blaring horns. I drove slowly around 30 kmph and gradually picked up speed joining the mainstream traffic. Ahead of me, a furlong or so, I could see the main traffic signal. Henry prompted, go straight ahead and at second traffic light, make a "U" turn and enter the parking lot in the same slot you came out from – T24 parking Slot. I meekly said "Yes" while concentrating on the thick traffic ahead of me. Since I was on the extreme lane, I had to carefully change over to the extreme left lane for the second U Turn. I was confident in my driving ability and at one point I imagined I was driving Angela's Camry without her on my right, instead, her father beside me! This thought produced a shy smile on my lips, and Henry said "Is everything OK". I answered politely "Yes "Henry smiled and just asked me, "Young man, what is your age like?" It was not a direct question about my age factor, but just a roundabout way of asking how old I was. I replied, "I am running on 30" and will be 31 in December. That answer satisfied him, and he politely said "I see "

Making a "U" Turn on the second signal was a bit tricky, as the road had small hawkers selling their wares, often, running behind the pedestrians persuading them to buy their goods. A taxi driver cut through my way, and

I narrowly avoided him, taking care not to hit the car on my left. I slowed down, as the traffic was high in numbers, and slowing down would either cause blaring horns or drivers hurling snarls at you! However, I kept my cool and concentrated, lowering down the radio volume a little bit. After the successful "U" Turn and changing of lanes, abruptly, Henry said to me, it was a clever maneuver. Pleased with Henry's observations, my confidence increased. "Drive the vehicle into the parking lot and park at T24" Henry said. I nodded my head and kept my eyes glued to the fast-moving traffic.

I slowed down very much upon entering the parking lot, trying to look at signs pointing to slot T24. Finally, I found the arrow leading to the curve of T24. I switched off the engine and closed the door gently, noticing the Camry was in Tip Top condition and wondered how Henry allowed me to drive his car without bothering to ask me if driving his car was OK or not? He was going to be — Inshallah *(borrowing ethnic terminology)* – my prospective Boss, but I had a right to my thoughts, isn't?

Climbing out of the escalator and back in his office, I noticed the interviewers had increased and some were gossiping amongst themselves. A hush fell immediately upon our entry, and Henry told me to go to the other room, freshen up, and answer some questions on a sheet carrying my name. I requested some water and coffee from the receptionist and she introduced her as Rosy, "P A to M D" It seemed she had an important role to play in the office management.

I refreshed myself and looked at the given questionnaire. Most of them were easy enough, yet there were some I had to read two times to understand the questions like

1.   Which Product is known as a Loss Leader?

2.   Company A sales are a million $, yet they are in Loss, whereas Company B has just Ten Thousand Sales, yet it has 100% Profits. Explain with an example.

I answered the questionnaire as best as I could and put the answer sheet in the given envelope, closed it, and returned to Rosy.

Exiting out of the interview room, thanking the receptionist, I caught the elevator going down and hailed a taxi which was parked along the side road. As soon I sat in the taxi, I checked my cell phone: there was a message from my mum wishing me Good Luck for the interview. There was also a missed call from Angela, and I knew it was a reminder for tonight's dinner date. I was eager to reach home and tell my mom about this strange interview!

Mom had just prepared evening Tea, as usual, when I reached home. Quietly, I freshened myself and joined Mom for tea. I described the interview episode and how I was asked to drive my prospective boss around his office area and the interview details. "Mom, surprisingly, he had a Camry car, and I was glad to drive it around, as you know, sometimes, I drive Angela's car". My mom did not like it, "What was the post you had applied for "? my Mom queried. Mom, the post was for an "Allrounder Accountant "and I don't think it matters, anyhow, I have done my best and hope for the best. Let's see what the result in the next few days is. I hope I am selected. I did like their office, and, if selected I would be glad to join them, as it seemed to be a nice place, in fact, their office was in the prestigious building, known as Merry Plaza, on Al Maktoum Road, overlooking Dubai Creek. The Company name MARGO ENTERPRISES FZE is an import export Company.

My mom made a point, Sunny (as my mother called me) he made you drive the car, just to observe you while "working". Your Accounting and Finance Jobs are too easy, armchair sit ins, just concentrating inside the 4 walls of the office, and not knowing anything happening in the real world. Figures, figures, figures and all that…. "Yes, Mom", I intervened, rightly thinking, I now understand. Henry had a couple of candidates in front of me, yet he chose to take me as an immediate candidate, and I remember, the others had their faces down, when I was being led out of the office door. True, he had camera scrutinizing visitors, but then, he did offer me a glass of water to break down my nervousness and start fast. "And Mom" I continued, I glanced at my CV in his hand, there were some pencil marks at certain places I noticed.

Yes, that's what I like, when I talk to my mom, she always has the third eye opened.

2. THE SECOND ANSWER

Was I late for my dinner- date? No, I don't' think so. Having tea with mom and resting a little really freshened me up. In fact, being a weekend, I was more relaxed, and having given an interview, relaxed me further. But there was still an uneasy feeling about a question I could not understand, though I had heard about the term before "Loss Leader ". Anyway, I cared a hang about it, let me go and see Angela and tell her "Guess who's Camry I drove today?". I wondered what her reactions would be!

I dressed up, wearing a smart Tee Shirt and Jeans. I rechecked my Tee Shirt: had it a front pocket, if no, then "No" outing with this Tee shirt. Yes, it did have a small pocket, cleverly hidden within the Zebra design marks on the front of the Tee Shirt. That is what I liked about it, the small frontal pocket is good enough to keep a tenor, or a Travel Pass, or just a neatly pressed Tissue. My self-examination over, I called Angella to say, I was leaving home and would be just at the café in 20 minutes time and she too should dress up and be there in 20 minutes time. She said she was fine and just leaving now. Happy at the reconciliation of time, I bade "Bye" to Mom, and set out. I think she was resting on the sofa and engrossed in watching TV

Heading to Café "SendMeLikes", near Grand Metro Station on Sheikh Zayed Road, I was eager to tell Angela about my interview and Camry driving experience! In a few moments, I will come to know. I knew she would park her beige Camry car on the roof top parking, of the same venue where this café is located.

The well-mannered waiter greeted me with a warm smile and inquired "Table for Two"? Yes, it is there at the far end of Coffee Shop. I reached the spot and pulled my chair, keeping my white tissue on the table in front of me. I wiped my glasses with the tissue and cleared the glasses, which had got dimmed upon entering the airconditioned café. In a few moments, I saw the café door opening and Angela entered, craving her neck to look out for me. I raised my hand up, and she came in my direction and sat opposite, after shaking hands. "Are you sitting in here for a long time? "She asked. "No, No, as a matter of fact, I just came a few moments ago" I replied. She asked "How are you, and how is Auntie? (meaning my mom). Is her health, OK? I said I and my mom are fine, and how are you, Angela? "Very Fine" she replied and sat down opposite me.

The waiter, who had greeted me at the entrance, peeped in, and from far, signaled his colleague to attend to us. I showed him my Thumb (suggesting "Like"). We, regulars at "SendMeLikes" do to assure our likeness for the café. Angela too raised her thumb. I asked her Do you want *"Thumbs Up* Or *"TEA"* We smiled, we laughed, we liked, We made a "V" sign with our Index finger and middle finger. Likes Like Likes.

So, Angela, how was your day? I asked. "I had my Arts Class today, and did some real good art work… my teacher was pleased and gave me more artistic work to do as homework. I love ARTS, and I take it to my h-e-ART. I liked that, I commented. Shall we order Tea / Coffee / Espresso/ or…, she called the waiter by raising her hand. And what shall you have, besides Tea? She asked. OK what comes after T? I asked. "U" comes after "T". Ok, you want Me? No, and Yes, I want Coffee and for you, shall I order Tea? or … yes, "O" for "Order" and we laughed. The waiter gave us a puzzled look and recommended Tea, Coffee, and Espresso to share in between along with Today's special snacks like, Spring Rolls, Sandwiches and Samosas. I said we are small eaters, just get us Samosas and spring rolls with Tea and Coffee, No Espresso….. but make it Express…. The waiter nodded and smiled and turned towards the kitchen area.

I was eager to tell her my experience of today, so I asked Angela "Where did you park your car today? She appeared surprised, and said in our building premises, of course!

It was then I teased her "You see, I drove Camry today, and I like the car. "Do you have a duplicate car key? she interrupted in between. "No, No, No way, I went for an interview at Al Maktoum Street today, and I narrated to her my whole episode. Surprisingly, Angela was calm, and then jokingly added "was it a Chauffer's Job Offer?". "More than that ", I replied and further described my interview with Henry. She seemed to be interested and yet had a look of disbelief on her face. I could understand that, as even my mother had disbelieved me in the beginning. Angela asked me," Well, Robin, what was the part of you driving Camry car? "Yes, I was a bit afraid of the assignment, but you know, jobs are difficult to get by, so I accepted Henry's order. Mind you, I became more confident after I saw the make of the car "Camry" and I immediately conjured you will be sitting next to me, and me driving! With that thought in mind, I got energized somewhat. Now, tell me Angela, how many times you have given me your car for driving, and have I ever met an accident or got any fines while driving. "Angela, my dear, you must be positive in your mind, else you will always remain in your comfort zone. Taking a risk does not mean you are welcoming failure; rather you are overcoming your fears: mind you these are my mom's words, and I always cherish her advice. Visibly comforted, Angela now appeared a bit peeved, I noticed. "Come on, let us grab our spring rolls, least they spring out from our plates! I whispered to Angela, to that she added, we are already in Spring Season, so let us enjoy our spring rolls, tossing a small piece of spring roll in my mouth. Cheers! I cajoled her into a lively mood, and she was now calm. Angela, you have also done your Commerce and Economic course: Tell me what or WHO is a Loss Leader. Promptly, she said "You" pointing straight into my face. I was surprised at her instant reply, and asked for an explanation. She said "You have always footed our outings, and never allowed me to pay for anything, so YOU are the Loss leader, smiling and letting her index finger point directly at me. I laughed at her silly sense of humor, but she became a bit serious, and replied" Yes, I know the term "Loss Leader". You see when, in a company, most products are yielding profits, yet some slow moving products are sold at a loss to cut down inventory, at the same time pushing slow- moving stocks out of inventory. "Brillant, Brillant, I echoed, Angela

FULL MARKS for You. You see, I knew something to this effect, but my mind went blank when I read this question in the interview with MARGOA ENTERPRISES FZE. Thank you, dear, for your very right answer.

"Are you still thinking about today's interview? Relax now, it is a weekend", Angela said. Truly, I recollected I was still agog with the sort of interview I got and the Big Boss, Henry's personality. In my mind, I was still thinking, why was I called, while other candidates were still waiting. And I also recalled the glare I got from the waiting candidates. But for now, I crossed my heart, and said to forget this chapter for the time being and enjoy the weekend. The waiter came forward and asked "would you like to have something else we have delicious caramel popcorn on offer, Sir. "Pop Corns" Angela beamed I want to take it for my POP. He loves it. I was half laughing and half thinking at the light heartedness of my girl, Angela, she was brainy, jocular, and above all very accommodating. "Yes" make it 2 portions of POP CORN, I too shall take it for my mother, it would be something of a change for her. So saying, we attacked our samosas. They were delicious but a bit spicy, I found, while she relished saying she likes it "hot and spicy"

Entering majestically a figure turned inside the café, a tall handsome man with broad chest, tugging along a pretty damsel, no less than an actress. All heads turned to see this pair get in, the waiters making a bee line to serve this handsome couple. As luck would have it, for a moment I though "Henry" had walked in –I was frightened to mention this to Angela, least she walks out of the café calling me a nerd or so. I moved my eyes from the couple and gazed at Angela's long flashy ear-rings. "Angela, you are wearing very long earrings, from where did you get? My Bestie presented me today, she returned from Hong Kong, yesterday. Jasmine is a real gem of a lady, so caring and loving, we get along very well. Thanks for noticing, dearie, you are also a Bestie! and she blew a kiss in the air. The conversation helped me enjoy the weekend.

I signaled the waiter to bring the bill and as soon as I said, Angela sprang to her purse, pulling from there a smaller wallet containing cash. This time, "I am going to foot the bill, and I don't want you to be a Loss Leader, she laughed. Again, she reminded me about the interview, and from the corner of my eye, i tried to crane my neck to see the guest who was a Look A Like of Henry. There he was at the far end and I saw him with his cell phone glued to his ear. By this time, the waiter had already collected cash from Angela and I felt sore about it. Angela protested, saying "Next time you pay, and I shall also bring my Bestie along with me, if you don't mind. You know Jasmine is a very lovable lady, even she likes my mom very much", she is a born sweetie. "Ok, done" next time please bring along her. How do we go now? Angela are you going to drop me, and let me drive your car, or …."Of course you are going to drive my Camry, and I like to be driven, giving me a mysterious look. Again she reminded me of my interview, which I was trying to forget. She sensed something was wrong and point blank asked me "Are you sure, you can drive, else, I can drive, as again, I shall have to get down and change seat". It is Ok, I can manage, I love driving you and your car….Aren't we made for each other, I laughed. So we moved to the parking lot and I spotted her car on the Rooftop Parking, when I pressed the ignition key, the car gave, a sort of blueish wink, distinctly different from the other cars lights. What is this now? I asked Angela, who also noticed twitching of my lips. A pleasant surprise, lets go, now. Soon, in about 30 minutes, we were at my place, and I alighted from the CAMRY and requested Angela to come up to my home and meet my mom. "Next time, sure I will, come to your house and meet your mom, and besides, I am just wearing a common dress. "You ladies, I growled, are always fussy about dresses, make up, and what not. "Yea" it is the GENDER difference, you know" and we both laughed. There you go, and she handed me the POP Corns packet and said, I think you forgot about it. "Yes", I am sorry. "You don't have to say sorry, I understand, and she gave a big broad smile and we patted each other's cheeks and wished goodnight. I stood watching her make a "U" turn and disappear in the thick traffic.

My mom was happy to see me return early, and she had just finished her light evening meals, and when I gave her Popcorns, she thanked me, for bringing "something different" as she put it. And mom what did you do, in the evening, I asked her. Our neighbor's little daughter dropped in, saying, she wanted me to read stories from children's book, and was not interested to go a movie, along with her parents. In fact, "Oh, look there, she forgot her story book on the table. I read the title of the book "Tales from A Rainbow's End Series 3 —King Larry Kills And is Petted" by Suresh Thadhani. "Hey, what a funny tittle : How can you be petted, when you kill somebody? My mom picked up the phone to ask Fionia, our neighbor, to collect the book her daughter left with us. I dissuaded her by telling her, I will be happy to read the book at night, before going to sleep.

3. Child – Like Mind

I got up at 6 O'clock in the morning. Prayed mentally, before getting up from the bed, as my usual practice. But something was ringing in my mind… a child's happy laughter, perhaps a dose of yesterday's late-night reading. Yes, it is true my mind said. Children are so cute, so happy and always smiling, lost in their own world, with not a care in the world: assured their parents and siblings will take care of everything. I was still drifting in thoughts, when I heard my mom's feeble sound of prayers. She was very religious, was much earlier riser than I. She had finished her toiletries and bath much before 5am. Then she would listen to recorded religious songs and sip her specially brewed tea, which spread the aroma in the kitchen. And since my bedroom was near the kitchen and prayer room, I could always get up in the early morning hours, but get up, of course a little later than mom. I stretched for a moment, got up, and rushed to the bathroom, taking care to tip toe the ground, not wanting my mom to know I had got up. My routine was: tooth brush, toiletries, bath, and finally prayers, and set out on the terrace for yoga or exercises, depending on my wish. Yes, I would collect the newspaper from the door front, drink the tea, which mom made and hand over the newspaper to my mom, before heading for the GYM on our rooftop.

Miss Bharati, the YOGA teacher, saw me and beckoned me join her group, sliding a spare yoga mat towards me. I smiled and joined the foursome who were doing yoga. Pleased with the morning brightness, and the entrusted zeal of Bharati, I felt my lungs expanding, with deep breathing exercises and yoga postures, I really felt energetic and how 45 minutes passed by, was a mystery to me. At the end of yoga session, Miss Bharati called me.

"Robin, you have got good physics, and I want you to do a little better. You see, when you bent down to touch your feet, you could barely touch your feet, and mid-way you lifted yourself. That is incorrect. "Would you mind doing with me now, for just 5 minutes, so that you get a hang of it?" "Gladly "I said, why not, Ma'am, it will be my privilege to be corrected and molded under your guidance. "Okay, let us go to the far end of this room, over the balcony side, and follow me. I did as I was told. "Now bend and touch your toes and hold it there" Bharati spoke in her soft voice. I did as commanded but could feel my fingers barely touching the toes. Thereupon, Bharati sat down cross legged and tugged my both hands with a gentle pull. "Ouch" I mentally cried, but she let her hands go, and told me to repeat 5 more times. I did as best as I could, but she caught my hands every time and gently pushed a little forward each time, making me more comfortable each time. On the 5th round I could do much better and could hold my hands on the ground. I was happy at her realistic training and got up to thank her. "Don't thank me, thank your body, Barathi said politely. And she continued

"Don't listen to your body, but rather convince your self by repeating in your mind "I can do it, I can do it, I will do it…. In that order, you will be able to do much better than expected. Body is the servant of the Mind, and it will obey at any cost, unless and until, it is in a defiance mood, and then your Anger erupts… Don't let that happen. "Oh, How Sweet, Bharati, you have made my day, Thank You So Very Much," I replied nodding my head. "So do I expect you at my Yoga Class, six days, a week, she coolly asked. Undoubtedly YES, I confirmed, as I was bowled over by her simplistic approach and advice. "Mam" just a question, "Why you said 6 days a week, and not 7 days a week? "Good Question", Bharati said, and continued, God made our wonderful world in six days, and the seventh day is a Rest Day ! Body needs rest too, though Mind is restless, as you know. "I was appalled at her wisdom and thanked her once again, taking her leave, Before, I turned to go, she causally said, Saturday, is my OFF Day and I won't be here. You too, Have a Good Day.

With exercises and good vibes, I felt more energetic and livelier, ready to face the day.

Mom had already made my breakfast of a club sandwich, consisting of omelet and green salad, mayonnaise and a strong hot cup of coffee. While enjoying my breakfast, I narrated to my mom, my yoga class with Instructor Bharati. My mom was pleased I was ordinated for 6 days of yoga under the care of Bharati. She knew Bharati as she quite often met her in the garden premise of our building, Bharati too knew her, but she did not know I was Maggie's son. My mother always introduced herself as Robin's mother, and not as Maggie, and this was the way it was. I told my mom about Bharati and her training.

She said she knew, in a distant way, Bharati, and really wanted to invite her in the evening hours, one of these days. I was happy to know this and prayed it would come soon. Mom, I shall be leaving for office within the next half an hour, as my Boss has said to buy some computer stationery for the office. Unfortunately, I forgot to buy yesterday, and somehow, today I will buy the items before reaching office. Oh ! yes, while I am returning from the office, would you want anything for me to bring. "No, not today, as I will be marketing on my own in the afternoon, just from the society stores, near the vegetables market." Would you be requiring anything, and what shall you want for dinner tonight? Mom, anything will do, just keep it to vegetarian level as I want to avoid meat of any kind. "Did Bharati tell you so?" my mom teased me. I laughed and went to dress up for the office. Mondays are very busy days, and sometimes office guests drop in, so I thought of wearing full sleeves white shirt and badge pants, and my Tie is always in my office cabin as I hate to wear Ties outside office. I also wore light brown socks to go with my badge-colored shoes. Taking a last glimpse in the mirror, I moved out of my room, saying bye to mom. Mom replied, with motherly care, sonny, have a good day and go with happy thoughts. That was her usual greetings, whenever I was leaving the house, and I did think of pleasant things to make my day cheerful.

Onwards to the Metro, I rushed to get the next train so I could have more time to buy computer stationery from my office area. As luck would have it, I got the 9.10am train and in 20 minutes I would be getting down at my destination and buy stationary items and be in time to office by 10 AM. With no other things to buy or look around, I gathered my items and went to the office. I was pleasantly surprised to see my Boss, Harilal Chanduram, earlier than I. Good morning, Sir, I wished him and entered my cabin. The office boy was cleaning my table, and I handed over to him the computer stationary to keep in the office cabinet. "Robin, the Boss was asking for pen drive, or USB, whatever you call, can I give it to him now that you have brought the stationary.

"Yes" do go and give him now, take 2 USBs as he needs a spare one too. My Boss was on intercom and said to see him after 15 minutes, as he would be leaving for a meeting. I remembered, last Saturday he had said he would be visiting a new client in South Dubai. I had a quick glass of water and decided to meet my Boss. My Boss was a remarkable man, he had an extensive memory and could recall details minutely. Not only that, he was very good at figures, and on the tip of his fingers, could calculate equally faster than the calculator. His vast memory and quick calculations netted good business contracts, and he even taught me many tricks of the trade, for which I was always grateful to him. This Monday, he had two meetings on the schedule, and I doubted if he would return to office before mid day.

"Robin, come here and take this USB, I have copied the files, and there is some data to be inputted from your side. As soon as you finish it, send me on my email, I will be with the client and see that you re-check the data before you send it to me. You can take help of Sheila, if you need to. "It is fine, OK, sir, I said and I saw Harilal disappearing from the office. I was now more relaxed, seeing the boss leaving the office.

I took a cup of tea and settled down to work on my assignment. It was just a routine job, and I did not think I shall need any help from Sheila. However, to be on the safe side, I shall re-check along with her, before scanning the documents and emailing. It took me nearly 45 minutes to gather the required information and analyze the data and cross check the totals and sub totals, There was a tiny error of a duplicate entry, the party had sent us a cash bill and also a credit bill for the same item, I reconfirmed from the party on phone, and Surya apologized for the error and told me he will sent me a credit note for the error. I was OK with that, and among the 30 odd entries, this was the only discrepancy found. Now, it stood corrected, and I was confident of my accounting. I called Sheila to scan the respective bills and file them date wise, making sure I had signed all the bills. She was quite efficient in her job and I wrote the needed email to my Boss. Other than this urgent job, I had on hand, some creditors accounts to be reconciled, and some follow up be done with our Accounts Receivables, particularly the aged debtors. Besides these petty reconciliations, I had to do Stocks Analyzing, to order fresh fast-moving items. This was a tricky job, as prices vary very fast and I did not want to block my cash flow in non-moving stocks. My Boss was very pleased with my Accounting and treated me very well in the office. All this was possible, as I had vast experience in practical handling of every aspect of accounts.

Sheila pressed on the intercom and asked me to speak to a bank customer, who wanted to know some personal details of our business. I told her these could be crank calls and she should tell the customer to write to us an email regarding his query. The line got dropped immediately, much to Sheila's relief.

We were nearing lunch time, and I asked the office boy to get a vegetable burger for me, I had decided to sit during the lunch time, least our Boss drops in and engages us for the day. Always, Mondays are hectic, and we office colleagues are mostly busy — I had also scheduled a Sales and Collection meeting around 2pm, that is after the lunch break. Sheila informed, our Boss would be in around 4pm, and I should convey the sales and collection meeting in his presence. That was much better, as Boss's presence always yields better results, I believed.

Sharp at 3.50pm the Boss was in. He freshened himself, and asked for a cup of tea and asked me to get all the sales staff ready for the meeting. Sunder, Raju, Joseph, Leena and David were already seated for the meeting, ready with their homework. Our Boss told us to come to the Meeting Room and each salesperson should present actual sales, collections updated, and budgeted figures. All sales staff had reached their Sales budget, but all lacked in Sales Collections, only Leena had 100% collections, with almost no sales. This was the conflicting point : If sales could go higher, than the collections suffered as traders seldom paid timely. Boss had made an effective statement : Less Sales not a problem, but 100% collections a MUST. This is the business policy and all have to toe the line, Boss warned. There was a long silence, and the Boss said : Make concrete efforts, determination is essential to succeed in life. The more you are determined, the more you will achieve. It was nearing 5pm and the meeting ended with an affirmation from all to do Better and Better.

Before returning home, I called my mom to know if she needed anything from the bazaar. She said she had done shopping in the afternoon, and she did not need anything. That was a relief, as going to the bazaar, was quite time-consuming job. Besides, I had decided to go for an evening walk. Reaching home, I freshened up and told mom, I would be going for a walk for about an hour, and then later come back for dinner. She agreed, saying she had cooked something special for me. I replied mom "all your food is special to me, I will like whatever you have made. Teasing me, she said, Ok, I have made brinjals, will you eat it? We laughed, as she knew very well I don't like brinjals!, come to think of it, brinjals are rated lower in caliber, or whatnot, and sometimes, I have heard expressions, like "this fellow is a brinjal (mutt). I left for the walk, still enjoying the sense of joke on me !

I had barely walked out of our building premises, when I spotted Bharati coming out from the garden area. I saw her and I said a "Hi" to her, she nodded, but continued to go in the direction of our building for, perhaps her Yoga classes.

My walk was through the outskirts of the garden area and beyond the main road, towards the beach. I could feel the coolness of the beach and hurried to cross the road by the overbridge. I like to go on stairs as I can see the beach more clearly, and from the height of the bridge, it was pleasant to watch beach goers : some jogging, some walking, some playing outdoor games, and still some others lying on the white sand. This scene always tended to be romantic for unknown reasons, and it was a mood changer, particularly after a hard day's work, hence I loved evening walks. As I walked on the sandy shores, I enjoyed seeing the lobsters being rolled out from the waves and jumping through the wet sand to reach the sea again. Their little red colored skin made a flashing wave in the twilight. At times, I could see some boats venturing into the sea for fishing. They would be out in the sea and return by early morning — unloading their catch in the nearby fish market. Yes, did my mother make a special fish- dish? I seemed to ask my mind.

I was right, reaching home I could smell the fish in the kitchen, and proudly proclaimed to my mother, that she had made fish for the night and I had nostalgia from the beach! She laughed and said "fish mongers" — do you know Angela is coming home tonight as a surprise visit? "How come, I asked "she did not tell me. "It is because, she called you, on landline, while you were in the wash room. I informed her you were in the wash room, she said, anyway, it is nice to talk to you Auntie. Jokingly I told her, why did you not drop at our place yesterday when you dropped my son home? Angela felt a bit peeved and apologized and said, she will certainly drop in today "just for some time" And she told me not to tell you, and let it be a surprise. "Oh! Oh! So you ladies have planned and "fished me out". "Good awkward thinking", and I hugged my mom for the favor and the disfavor ....

Angela came around 8pm, wearing a nice navy blue dress, and carrying a basket of fruits. Why did you bring that? my mother queried, pointing at the fruit basket. "It is especially for both of you, as I know you both love fruits." "Thank You, Thank You" we both said in unison and sat down on the sofa. The clock chimed 8 times and reminded us to get ready for supper. The ladies disappeared into the kitchen bringing a tray of fry fish, pasta, salad, and some soft drinks. It was a light supper and we all ate cheerfully… Angela was asking my mom for the receipt of "Lemon & Spiced Fry Fish" It tasted delicious, and I could hear everyone saying "yummy, yummy, but I said "mummy, mummy", and Angela gave a burp with laughter. The food was over in 15 minutes, and Angela asked for leave, as her mother was alone in the house, her father always returned late from his business, she said. While leaving, my mom gave Angela some custard and jelly, which she gladly accepted. At the corner of the exit, Angela asked me "Any news of the interview you gave? ""Not yet" I replied.

I wore slippers and carried her takeaways, to accompany her to the parked car. She was in a hurry, as she had forgotten to check her parking time. She did not want her dad to be surprised with a parking ticket. She bade Bye to me and said "Dream you have got the new job. Dream you are sitting in your new office and learning newer things, Good Luck, and she turned on the ignition and waved out leaving me staring at her speeding car.

My mom was delighted with Angela's visit and being tired, we both went to sleep.

4. THE WAKE-UP CALL

I usually get up from bed in a jiffy. I don't laze around, but before touching the floor, I curl my foot fingers and stretch out arms briskly, Thanking the Almighty and repeating "Thank You God, for the Good Health and well-being You have given to me and my family" I repeated this small prayer several times in the bathroom. I could hear my mom's movement, probably, in the kitchen, preparing tea and breakfast. Coming out of the wash room, I went straight to the Prayer room and finished my prayers — I don't know why— but a sentence popped in my head "You have got a new job". For a moment, I was puzzled and looked around me, no one was near me, only I was staring at the statue of Mother Mary. "Robin your cell phone is ringing, my mom called. I rushed to pick up the call, not guessing who the early morning could be. A pleasant voice greeted me "Good Morning, am I speaking to Robin" the female voice at the other end called. "Yes, Good Morning, who is this, please? "I am Rosy, the receptionist from Margoa Enterprises FZE, could you please visit our office anytime today, but not later then 4pm" and she paused for my answer. Without thinking, I answered "Yes, Yes, sure enough I will be there before 4pm ". Alright then see you, Bye' the female voice cut off the line. "Mom", I called "Mom, Mom, please come here, there is good news. "Rosy called and asked me to see her in her office before 4pm. "Sonny, is this your new girlfriend, you seem to be so excited? "Mom, this is no tomfoolery, Rosy is the receptionist of MARGOA ENTERPRISES FZE, the office I went for interview, last week. "Oh! that is so nice, now I recollect, but was not that office far off… Jebel Ali in South Dubai? Yes, mom, but she was kind enough to let me come today, late afternoon, else who cares to ask you like that? I think I will take a half day from my Boss and tell him I am not feeling well and carry on for the interview "Never say, you are ill, sonny" respect your body, just give him any other excuse, you know body listens to your mind, and you might really feel ill "Cross out that thought. Breakfast is ready, have it soon, the tea is getting cold. I thanked Mom for her wisdom, and inwardly recalled, the exact words of Bharati, who too advised me the same. *Your Body is the servant of your Mind…*

OK, mom, I shall tell my Boss some other excuse, no worries. I shall eat the breakfast now,

My mind wavered, was I being called alone, or else would there be some other candidates too? I hit my forehead and promised no more negative thoughts, just carry on. Whatever must happen, will happen. Just before leaving the house, I once again went to the prayer room to seek Lord's Blessings.

I reached my office and found no one had arrived yet. Good, I could plan out today's work schedule and see to it I am able to release myself from office, at least by lunch time. I opened my diary and made a work flow chart:

yes I would be able to finish my current jobs on hand, by noon time. When Heeralal, my big boss would come, I would tell him my uncle has come from abroad, just for 2 days, and has a busy schedule, but has willed to come to our place today noon, so I need to meet him. That was the best simple reason I could think of. Like that, Heeralal was quite understanding and was quite fond of me, as I have worked for him for more than 9 years here. Many of the staff have changed the employment within one year, or so.

I did my day's work quite diligently, but often kept on looking at my watch. Sheela, our office secretary, popped in our accounts department and asked me what could we be ordering for lunch, as usually we share lunch together. I told her my uncle has come from abroad —just for 2 days– and I shall be leaving at lunchtime as I must meet him. She said "Oh No, then, I shall order a small portion, only for me" and she moved out from our department. Ranjeet, the sales guy, told her not to worry, as he would be bringing something for her, whilst on his outdoor job. Ranjeet had overheard my conversation and knew, any moment I would be leaving now. I called Sheela and told her I have already sent an SMS to Heeralal and he has acknowledged too. I left the office, picking up my Tie and neatly folding in my pant pocket. Sheela noticed but did not comment. I wished her bye and left for the Metro.

In the Metro Plaza I had eyes to scan the name MARGOA ENTERPRISES FZE only,,,,, just to recollect the floor. This time I took I lift and headed to office 206. Maria was expecting me anytime now, and had already few papers in her hand. But she called me in her ante room, calling Rosy to take her seat in her absence. The dark skinned lady, whose name I knew now, composed herself on the chair and with the bright light facing her face, she looked smart enough to be a receptionist.

"Listen carefully to what I say now, Rosy responded staring hard in my eyes "You have been selected : CONGRATULATIONS AND WE WELCOME YOU TO MARGOA ENTERPRISES FZE!"

For more on our company business, please visit our www mentioned on the letterhead. We have our offer letter ready. Please read the Terms and Conditions, before we go further. If you agree, we will go further, and she handed me the "Letter of Appointment" to read. After you have read the letter, please sign the copy and take the original with you.

I paused and lowered my eyes on the letterhead. The first thing that attracted me was the salary figure they offered me Dirhams Eight Thousand plus Travelling Allowance of Dhs One Thousand. It made me very happy, and I mentally blew a whistle. My first thoughts were: how happy would my mom be! My poor mom had been leading almost on poverty lines, and this figure was a very desirable figure compared to the miserable all told salary and allowances of Dhs 4000/- with the *Kanjoos (miser, in Indian language)* Harilal, the owner of Paradise Import and Export Ltd…… surely he has now exported me! I beamed with joy… suddenly Rosy asked "Have you finished reading the letter, and do you have to say anything? Rosy could feel my inner happiness, but she suppressed all emotions, remaining stoic. Here was a lady in front of me who could be dealing more with me, as upfront manager, as she was PA to the Boss. "Thank You Rosy, I have signed the copy and retained the original with me. As you need to know my starting date with you, I prefer to join you from the first of next month, that is barely 14 days from today. Is that all right, as I must discharge my work responsibilities from my current employer. "It should be Okay with us "I shall inform Mr. Henry. Before you leave, I need you to meet Santosh, our HR manager, who will let you know the joining procedures and the visa formalities. "OK" I said, and she lifted the phone and spoke on intercom: Mr Robin is here, would you like me to send him to your office, if you are not busy. "I am on a call now, please send him to me after 10 minutes" and he hung up the phone. I could hear every word of the conversation as Santosh's voice was loud and clear. Rosy pointed to the sofa and asked me to sit down. I scrolled my eyes around the walls and could see some certificates and photos of some meeting hung on the opposite walls. I wanted to examine the contents, but dared not to do so, as it could be impolite, I thought. In a few moments, a tall man with tie and a full suit came and looking inquisitively at me, stood a little away from me, until Rosy came to the rescue and introduced him to me saying "this is Robin, our new recruit, and looking towards me, she said Robin, this is our HR Manage, Mr Santosh. We shook hands, "How long have you been in Dubai, young man" Santosh politely asked me. "Well" Sir, I am here in Dubai, since July 1976. "Oh! I see, then you must know about Employment Visas", to process it we will need your original certificates, duly stamped by UAE Authorities, along with your original passport, an NOC from your present employer. Get it ready and leave with Rosy, asap and he left, saying, he is expecting some calls and would take our leave. The meeting was dispersed, and

I set sail homewards, saying "Bye' to Rosy, and carrying carefully holding the envelope containing my Letter of Appointment.

I was too excited to show my appointment letter to my mom. How happy she would me upon seeing the contents. Good God, at least one sock of poverty will be removed, God willingly. Wait a minute, why did I not see Henry in the office? It did not even occur to me to ask Rosemary about our Big Boss ! How stupid of me. Anyway, the injustice was done, now no regretting. In my quizzical thinking, I had overstepped the Metro Station and I retraced a few steps back, shaking my head a little bit.

5. Smiles and Sorrows

Robin's mother washed her moist eyes. She did not remember how long she was praying until she happened to watch the clock in the gangway chiming 11 o'clock. Today was the death anniversary of her late husband, Mario Mark. Ever since he was gone, she had a very tough time in her life. In around three months' time, with income gone and savings dwindling, she managed to take up part time jobs, tuitions to the children, garment making contracts with the tailors, home cooked snacks to school canteens, et al. Yet, God was very kind to sail her through life's storms. Robin was only two years old and did not understand life's strategies. And she had promised herself, not to let Robin grief or remorse about her being a one parent family. Whenever little Robin asked her about Dad, she would say, he is abroad and working in an office in Japan, a very far off place.

Today, she had decided to go to church, in the evening with Sonny. There was a call on her mobile, and, since she was in the middle of prayers, she ignored the call. She asked forgiveness for any mistakes she or her sonny had made inadvertently. She felt peace in the solitude of her home. Again, the phone rang, and she once again decided to ignore it and see later who the caller was, after her prayers were over in a few minutes of time.

She knew it would be her sonny, and she was right. She dialed his number and she could hear his panting on the phone: she was abruptly shaken at the sound she was listening: Mom, Mom, very good news, I have been selected by MARGOA ENTERPRISES FZE, and you know what, they have offered me double of my present salary, nearly a five digit figure per month. It is Nine Thousand Dirhams … "What?" her mom queried in dis belief. "Sonny, God has answered our prayers, today, in the evening we are going to the church, you and me, as also, is your dad's anniversary (she deliberately avoided the word D…). "Yes, mom, I do remember, and in the morning, I saw his photo you had kept beside, Mother Mary's statue. It is his Blessings from Heaven, and she could feel the tears in her son's eyes. She ended the call by saying, bring some flowers, for the church, on your way home.

Robin bought a bouquet of flowers, sweets, and sugar-coated bread rolls from the market for today's visit to the church.

The doorbell rang, and little Jovina was at the door asking for her storybook which she had forgotten yesterday. Then she silently turned to go to her apartment, saying "Bye" to Robin's mother. Robin got out of the lift and saw little Jovina. He called Jovina and petted her forehead and offered a sweet sugar roll which she gladly ate. She asked for a flower from the bouquet. Mrs. Mark called out from the doorway, "Sonny give her one, children are Angels "and I am sure the church will pardon us for shop lifting from the bouquet". Nobody understood a word of her sentence, but mom believed a shadow came from nowhere, and blessed them. "Amen" I heard my mom say.

The corridor of St. Mary's Church was overcrowded, but we made the way to the Alter. Gently placing the bouquet of flowers, I knelt down and prayed, My mom just behind me, with eyes closed and in quite reverence prayed, her lips moving slowly. We could feel the sprinkling of Holy water by the priest and there was an aroma of scent from many flowers being brought in by the worshippers. As the crowd was thickening, we turned and made our way out the church. At the gates of the church, were little urchins seeking alms, and my mom gladly gave bread rolls to the needy. With a sense of moral achievement, we left homewards. In a few moments we were back home and I showed my Appointment letter to my mom. She went over it, and I could notice tears of Joy — and sorrow— oozing out of the corners of her eyes. My mom, inquired, when I would be joining Margoa…. I replied, I had committed to them, my joining date as first of the next month, barely two weeks from today. She asked, how about your present employment? Would they accept just a half- month notice? I replied "mom, I will have to face the situation, I can't risk losing this valuable offer, if worst comes to worst, I will re imburse them my half month's salary. I don't think Harilal will be that nasty, let us hope and pray for the best.

Next day, was going to a tension day, I thought in my mind. I had to write my resignation letter, update all my jobs, explain to Harilal I am resigning, and wait for his reaction. There was no fear on my work front, my job was easy and any commerce graduate with some five years' experience would be able to manage the show. My thoughts were interrupted by a gentle knock on the door. Who could this be? I peeped from the eye hole and saw a lady in white. In the darkness of the passage, I could not see clearly, however, I opened the door and saw Bharati waiting at the door! "Oh! Oh! It is you, Robin, Bharati explained, I am looking for the apartment of Mrs. Mark, would you be knowing her apartment? "Yes, please you are at the right place, I live here with my mom, Mrs Mark. I am her son. Please step in"

Hearing the noise at the door, my mom peeped out of her bedroom and upon hearing Bharati's voice, she welcomed her in eager tones "Bharati, Oh! Bharati, welcome to our house, for a long time I was thinking of inviting you, but some how or the other, I keep forgetting the thought. I am glad you took the liberty of visiting me. "Robin is your son? I did not know that, good I am meeting 2 people in one go. "Go, you won't, rather come in, Bharati, my mom cheerfully replied. I switched on the air-conditioner and brought a glass of water, lighting up the corridor light too. Now, in the clear bright light, I could see Bharati, my YOGA teacher. I was as happy as my mother upon meeting Bharati. "I knocked on your door for a specific reason : I am having a FREE YOGA CLASS, in your building on the coming Sunday, after a request from senior members of this building through the property Manager, Mr. Das Gupta, my oldest student of this building. So, here I am. "That is very kind of you, Bharati, as old age creeps on, you do need soft exercises for your body, I feel. "You are quite right, especially, the breathing and mediation in Yoga sessions, really freshens you up. Stealthily, I moved out of the room to prepare a cup of tea for all of us. Sometimes, when you ask the guest for tea or water, generally they say "No", but when you place in front of them they tend to take the offer, respecting your hospitality. "Robin is an excellent Yoga disciple and I always feel is steadily improving "He has assured me six days dedicated practice and I am quite happy about it. And now, that I know, he is your son, I shall take extra care to boost him up, cooly replied Bharati. My mom was fascinated with Bharati's talks and assured her that on the coming Sunday, we would join her for her special YOGA Class. The discussion now turned on ladies topic, and I excused myself to draft my resignation letter. I heard my mom telling Bharati she would go down with her for a small walk and know more about each other. That suited me as I needed to concentrate on my job on hand.

Within thirty minutes, I cleared my room, refreshed myself, and wrote my resignation letter. I re – read the few lines I had written, thanked the management in the letter and realized about nine years, I had been working for them. I had learnt a lot from the management, gathered valuable business knowledge, did full fledged accounting and introduced many accounting and store keeping procedures, bringing the company from basic accounting to polished accounting. We had regular Audits, obtained, ISO 9001 & ISO 14001 certificates with my team of accountants and my senior colleague, Mr Krishna Murthy. At a point of time, I did feel sad about leaving the family-like atmosphere, but our Big Boss, Hiralall, was way too miser. He would give us yearly bonuses, yet not increments, as he knew his liabilities would grow with increased salaries. I put a stop to my thinking and went to see my mom and Bharati. My mom had sent me an SMS on my mobile saying she was going for a walk with Bharati. I had kept my mobile on silence and did not notice the message earlier. My mom had written, she would be back by 7.30pm and now it was already 7.15pm

Mom arrived, looking fresh from the walk. I showed her my R- letter and she wished me good luck. We knew, at a point of time in everyone's life, cutoffs creep in, and we must accept the realities. Well, this was my asking, and I knew it.

Once again, Mrs. Mark marked another day in her life: Sorrows And Smiles, God's Plans.

6. New Beginings and Newer Clothings

"Good Morning, Sheela, how are you this morning?" I said cheerfully upon entering the office. "I am fine sir, and how are you, Robin? she replied. I was feeling happy inwardly but still a bit nervous at breaking the ice about my resignation. To smoothen things, I asked the office boy, Ramu, to get a hot cup of tea. "Yes, Sir, in an instant" and he disappeared. Not to lag behind, Sheela called out "Ramu, for me, a coffee please. I shall drink with Robin. We often gossip over a cup of tea, and I welcomed Sheela in my cabin. At the same time, Krishna Murthy walked in, and seeing us in one cabin, asked if he could join, else… "Good Morning, Krishna, very much welcome, join us for tea, and Sheela yelled, "Ramu, 2 Teas and one coffee, please. "Coming, coming mama, soon "Ramu replied.

Krishna told us he is enrolling in a car driving institute as he is tired of train journeys. "It is a welcome step", I added. Sheela mischievously added, "Ah, Yes" I can get a free lift everyday as I live in the same locality! "That is right", but do you know how difficult it is to get a driving

"

license in Dubai? I understand, said Sheela, but see Robin, he says he got the DL in the first attempt. "That is true' Robin said, but do you know, I deliberately took 50 lessons, with Star Driving Institute, a very good institute, they give you thorough lessons, and you pass successfully after a lot of driving practice ! Ramu, opened the door with his foot, balancing the Tea tray cautiously, and pushing his shoulders to get in the cabin. Sheela pulled the door towards herself, and Ramu settled the tea tray on Robin's table. Instead of moving out of the cabin, Ramu paused, and whispered: "Robin Sir, your tie is missing from your drawer, I noticed, while cleaning your cabin. Sheela stared in my face. I lowered my face and looked the other way around. Krishna gulped down his tea and left, saying he must catch up with his work. Sheela left the cabin shrugging her shoulders, avoiding eye contact.

I carefully switched on my computer and read the incoming emails, still wondering over the statement of Ramu. Only Sheela had noticed I took away the Tie from my drawer. Did she think I told a fib about going to meet my uncle, and needed early leave from the office?

I checked the incoming emails for any urgent replies needed, but most of them were for sales inquiries, being "cc" to me for information. There was only one important email from my boss, asking me to work on the costing of an export project for Ghana. Yes, I would attend it, but first I had to print my resignation letter and keep it in my drawer to show to Harilal. This done, I got busy with office routine.

Sheela announced on the intercom, Boss was coming in an hour's time and would want "Ghana Order Costing". I said I am aware of it and the file copy is being sent to him on his email, in few minutes. That over, I again checked my resignation letter and neatly filed in a flat file to present to my boss.

Harilal came in, and took off his coat and asked me "how is your uncle, did you have a gala time with him? "Yes, Yes' I replied, my uncle is fine, and we did enjoy the evening" "Good", my boss replied. "Thank You", I politely replied.

The "Ghana Order Proposal "was a tricky one. The party wanted quite a huge quantity of building materials, and hinted, repeat orders, for the next six months or so, provided we were the best bidders. My comments to Harilal was the items were in great demand, and market conditions were unsteady at the moment, we should not go for in for a "locked prices" order, we could be on the losing end in the long run if the prices increase in a short duration. Anyway, the boss had to decide, and he was a shrewd business, never in loss, on any order. I had a pleasant meeting on the subject, with options "A" and option "B"—Hiralal thanked me and told me to leave him alone for the moment. My mind was wavering as back of it I was thinking about my proposed resignation letter to be given to Harilal.

Walking out of my bosses' cabin was a relief as his room was very cold throughout the day.

After the lunch hour, I had decided to meet my boss and give him R letter, as food in the stomach relaxes a person, I believed.

Around lunch time, I noticed Krishna Murthy was in Harilal's cabin. I waited for the guy to come out and then

I could approach the boss. Sure enough, he came out in 5 minutes. With a file in my hand, I requested my boss to see him for a moment. Cheerfully, he said "come in" and I sat opposite him. Straight to the point, I handed him my letter, waited for him to read. "Robin, how long you have been working for me?' ""About "Nine years", I replied. "Ok" he continued, "Is that your final decision?" "Yes" I replied.

He looked straight in my eyes, and said "It is Okay with me", shall look out for another Accountant, when will be your last working day, here? This was the question I was dreading. "End of the month, Sir." Alright, what about the notice period, I think you are supposed to be here for one month after you have tendered your letter, isn't? "Yes, Sir, but I am requesting you to release me early as I have got a new job offer and I have decided to join them by first week of the next month" "OK" then, I do not want to come in your way, if you are happy with that, so be it ! You have worked hard and sincerely, I know that, so it is better to part happily. He called Sheela on the inter com and told her : Robin has resigned, please put a advertisement for a senior accountant post asking candidates if they could join us immediately. Then, looking at me, he said "Robin, I expect you to hand over your assignments to the new candidate, and train him for a few days, I hope it should be Okay, for both of us. Check up with Shrikant Shinde, my legal advisor.

Sheela disappeared quietly, as she had come in, requesting me to help her with the advertisement wordings, for the post of Senior Accountant. "I said" yes, I will and I too came out of the cabin, leaving Harilal alone, looking upwards towards the ceiling.

This meeting took the pressure off me, and I realized, Harilal, though stingy by nature, did not obstruct my leaving him. I should say he was kind enough to let me go in two weeks' time, not asking for any deductions from my salary. Sheela told me she would see me a bit later as she had some jobs tied up upfront. I agreed without any fuss, in the meantime, I could draft the wordings for the post of a senior accountant for an import export company. There were dime a dozen vacancies for accounting posts, and I was sure we could hire one and release myself from this office earlier than expected. I sorted out he day's jobs on hand and informed Krishna Murthy about the way I would be moving: keep him in the loop of my every office activity and making a note of it in my diary for backup information, He was quite nice and understanding, being my junior by thee years, in experience and age.

Sheela came in and looked somewhat sad. I showed her the advertisement wordings, and told her to insert in the newspaper under "Situations Vacant "in the leading two newspapers in Dubai. She asked me, if she could canvas in her friend's circle too. I said go ahead, as we needed the post to be filled as early as possible. She had someone in mind, and suggested could she ask Harilal for approval for the interview. I said you could always speak to Harilal, as there was no harm in trying. She was satisfied with my answer, but longed to know, where was I joining. Indirectly, she asked me, "will you keep in touch with us, once you are gone? " "Not immediately, but shall catch up with you guys sometimes, sure enough. Afterall, we have been colleagues for many years, I replied. She smiled, and added "we will all miss you". Yes, I know, so will I, not lifting up head from the paper work.

It was nearing five o'clock and I was still deciding to sit late or not, when I saw Harilal leaving the office. That set me good — I shall put in an hour more, and try to re organize my files, and suitably arrange in a logical order, so a new person can get ease of handling. I saw Krishna and Sheela leave together, but Ramu chose to sit behind, assuring me of an extra teacup, if I would care for one. Oh! Yes, anytime is tea-time, please get me one now, trying my best to be alone and pay attention to my work load.

Ramu came, brought a piping hot tea cup and politely sat across me, observing me working silently. "Yes, Ramu, something bothering you, come on with it. I am still here till the end of the month. "Sir, I shall miss you, you have always helped me in lot of ways, and I can't forget it. I am really sad, you are leaving us. "Is your new job in Dubai only, or you are moving out somewhere. "Ramu, I shall be in touch with you, occasionally, now please let me work in solitude. "Yes Sir, I am leaving now, I still did not find your tie, and he quietly left me, injuring me with an unknown guilt. It occurred to me, the other day, Sheela had noticed me wearing the tie and going out early : perhaps for an interview, she guessed, and my saying "I want to meet my uncle coming from abroad" did not buy the story ! She had even perhaps told others too, including Hiralal, who had appeared cool when I was discussing about my resignation. "Yes" I said to myself, this is office politics, the germ of insecurity in the office.

My cell phone rang, and I guessed it would be my mother asking me when I am returning. I was wrong: it was Angela, laughing and teasing me, "would you want an office assistant, I am available, but right now, am waiting for you "— please call me, when home and she disconnected, perhaps driving on a busy road ! I guessed.

7. Secrets Cannot be Bottled Up

I expected mom to be happy and asked for what would she want as a treat? (she never does), so I told her : How about going out for dinner tonight? And, if you so desire, we can call Angela and invite her too. Not a good idea, she said. You see, first start your job, earn your first salary, and then we can really celebrate. Yes, if you want, you can tell Angela to join us for dinner and share the good news. I have noticed she is always happy to come to our house. Mom, Angela, last time told me she is busy in the evenings, as she has joined an Arts Class, somewhere near her house, in Karama. Okay, then we too shall have dinner and go early to bed. Mom said. Being tired and excited I thought it was a good idea. There was a ring on my cell phone. I picked up and it was Sheela on the line. Hello, I said, everything OK, Sheela said, sorry to disturb you, there is a friend of mine, an accountant, can I call him for an interview tomorrow, if you do not mind. I was a little taken back. Sheela was never so personal with me, yet she just called me to get an interview for her colleague. However, I blindly said, yes, call him tomorrow around 11 am. She thanked me and hung up. Soon, it was bedtime and I went to sleep telling mom "goodnight": She was watching the TV

Getting up early in the morning, I searched for the newspaper, scanning the "situations vacant ", checking if our advertisement had appeared. Yes, there it was : in big bold type. Sheela forgot to mention "call after 10AM" and I knew there would be chaos in the morning, anyway I could not help it now. Finishing my bath and breakfast, I told mom I am going a bit early, expecting a busy day ahead. She appeared from the doorway and just said "Bye, go with Happy thoughts". I thanked her and closed the door from behind.

Surprisingly, Ramu was not in the office: usually he is the first one to come. I dusted my desk and opened the laptop, cleaning its screen. There was a ring on the board line. I did not pick, imagining it would be a "vacancy call". This was Sheela's job and I concentrated on the notes in my diary. Instead of Ramu coming in, it was Sheela who came in, a bit earlier. After the greetings, she said "Raj Sikander, will be coming in for an interview around 11 am, please favor him if you find him suitable amongst other candidates, it will be a personal favor to me". I did not reply to her but just waved my hand towards her. Sheela went to her seat and saw Ramu come in. Ramu apologized for being late as he missed the earlier train.

"No worries, Ramu" I said, just get along with the routines, and then my tea, please. "Yes, Sir" he beamed and disappeared in the pantry. "Sheela, when the calls for interview pour in, please short list them with a time slot of one hour in between. I shall take no more than 5 or 6 interviews today, beginning from 11 am onwards. I have important jobs to finish, as you know. "Yes, understood", Shella replied. In the first instance, send candidates to Krishna Murthy, whom I have already informed, to take the interview, and shortlist before sending the candidates to me.

Ramu brought the tea, along with today's newspaper. I marked our advertisement in a red circle and returned to Ramu, telling him to give it to Krishna Murthy.

I had closed my cabin door and was working closely with the Ghana Project papers. Re- checking the figures, I assured myself Harilal will be pleased as I had also made three versions of its calculations called scenario 1, scenario 2 and scenario 3. Sheela called me on the intercom saying Raj Sikander had come. I requested her to send him to Krishna Murthy and then later to me. She immediately obliged and led Raj to Krishna Murthy's cabin. I assured Sheela I would certainly see Raj after his interview was over with Krishna Murthy. Meanwhile, three other candidates had entered our premises and Sheela was busy attending to them, giving them forms to fill in along with test paper. She informed Ramu to keep some water bottles on the far end of the pantry room & if someone needed one, Ramu could always fetch them from there. Krishna called me on the intercom and said he is sending me Raj Sikander's papers with Ramu. Reading through the remarks of Krishna, and seeing the test paper, I concluded Raj could stand a chance and asked Sheela to send him to my cabin. Raj Sikander was a tall thin guy, with a fine line of moustache. He seemed to be in mid-thirties and appeared quite shy. "what is the present post you are currently having?' I inquired of Raj. "Sir, currently I am unemployed, just last week my company terminated me due to slow business, rest assured, I can handle company accounts very well. I was not inclined to interview him further as Krishna had already taken his interview. Cautiously, I called Sheela on the intercom and advised her to call this candidate tomorrow by that time I could have a word with Harilal. She sounded happy and requested Raj to have some water and leave for now. Raj thanked me and left without glancing at anyone.

After a few hours, I asked Krishna, how was the interview going so far? He seemed not to be pleased with anyone on academic grounds: most of the candidates had no bookish knowledge and were unable to answer simple questions. Krishna said, one day is too soon to decide, and he would prefer to interview more candidates in due course of time.

Harilal walked in, looking around the seated candidates, hoping someone was found suitable. I came out of the cabin, and told Sheela, I would take CV of Raj Sikander and talk to Harilal before the end of the day. Sheela nodded and just whispered "Thanks"

Harilal called me to come with the Ghana documents and see him soon. I saw Ramu take coffee to the room of Harilal and decided to see join Harilal, taking along Raj Sikandar's CV.

Harilal asked me if Krishna had seen this project papers, whereupon, I said "Yes, in fact we have analyzed the scenarios together and he is fully aware of the proposal." Let him finish interviews and when he is free, he can join us"

Harilal glanced at the documents, opened his laptop and reviewed the procurement of materials and sales. : Look, Robin, we have to allow some margin for the buyer to make a profit on few items, else he will not give us any business, and to cover up for loss on those items, we need to increase price of some items, or inflate freight cost to give us same margin of profitability. Plus, one more thing, we shall give him a rebate on sales, provided he achieves a certain target. Failing his target will not entitle him to our rebate scheme, understand. We shall add this clause. What do you think about it, Robin? "A brilliant idea, Sir", I responded. Technically, this catch is known as a "loss Leader" in our accounting terminology! I appreciate your theory knowledge, Robin, our entire family of businessmen from KUTCH, Gujarat, India are well known for trade and commerce. We have a saying : Let the skin go, but not the money… or in English how you say "Money Makes the Mare go" With a little laughter in the air, I paused and pulled out CV of Raj Sikandar. "Sir, this candidate is good enough for our employment, also he has done his test paper very well, besides our Sheela knows him, and has recommended him. "Call Sheela here" Harilal retorted. I lifted the side intercom and called Sheela to walk in. "Yes Sir, you called me." "Yes" please sit down, pointing to the opposite sofa. "Sheela, who is this candidate and how do you know Raj… "Sir, he is my brother's friend, occasionally, we meet in our compound, and he just mentioned to my brother he has lost his job, last week. Knowing there is a vacancy in our office, I spoke to by brother to ask him to send us his CV. In fact, I brought his CV with me yesterday and gave to Robin, sir ……Harilal cut me short the second time " OK" what salary he is expecting? Harilal asked me to go through the candidate's CV and update him later. I don't' encourage anyone to join us, if he knows you or any of our staff. "Known people, become a liability in the long run, that is why I even don't keep my own relatives in my company. I am sorry, Sheela you have to say "NO" to him, besides, if he joins us in our salary grade, he will be hunting jobs and not concentrating on job front. Our business community gives employment opportunities to hard working persons, who eventually gather rich experience with us. Harilal's tone was a bit high not realizing some candidates were waiting outside and could be listening to our talks.

Sometimes the truth is bitter, and Harilal, got up, and said he has more meetings and is leaving now, asking Robin to re do the figures of the Ghana Project.

Some candidates had left, perhaps eavesdropping, or tired of waiting. Krishna came to me and handed me three more CVs telling me, they were of average grade. Since we were not paymasters, we had a tough tug of war with the candidates, I felt. I still felt Sheela's contact would be suitable as he was quite up to the mark. I decided to speak to Sheela after lunch.

Today, it was Krishna Murthy's day to bunk: he came up to me and said his relative is leaving for UK and he needs to drop him off at Dubai Airport. And then, since there were some candidates expected in the allocated slot, I decided to skip lunch, if needed, I told Ramu to order a Pizza with potato wedges, from the downstairs Pizzeria, and I could share with him and Sheela. Ramu loved pizzas and rolled his tongue in his mouth, ready to go down after receiving cash from me. Sheela was in an off- mood and refused to have pizza with us. I convinced her to join me, stating I had a rethinking on Raj Sikander's case. A bit cheerful now, she smiled and said "OK, I shall join you, provided you allow me to pay for pizzas, I don't like it, as you always pay. I agreed unwillingly, clearing the stalemate.

One more candidate turned up, and I took his interview, as Krishna was just leaving. The candidate was highly qualified and had seven years post graduate experience. When I reviewed his CV, I found his current salary was over Dirhams Eight Thousand. Surprisingly, he told me point blank, he would not accept any salary lesser than his current salary. I had to let him go, as there was no point in having a halfhearted interview, Ramu was kind enough to offer him a glass of water, but the candidate refused making a face and looking wild. He left us perplexed commenting "he had come to a wrong company"

The arrival of pizzas cheered us up! Ramu told me to give his share of lunch, he could go to pantry and have it there. It made sense and Sheela sat in my cabin and opened the pizza box. After a quick meal, Sheela asked me if I could convince Harilal to employ Raj. Point blank I replied "Harilal, does not care for relationships in employment, only he wants least salary demanding candidate. Once a candidate joins us, he is tied up with the contract and cannot leave us for two years. And Harilal will not give a raise in between as you know, the candidate will automatically adjust to our system, and carry on till two years, or else till he gets a golden break elsewhere. This is the way the small businessmen work, they don't care as long as their work is being done. Sheela held her tea cup tightly, raising up to her mouth, gulping and got up, leaving me with her unfinished pizza slice. In my mind, I tried not to be sidetracked by my own views.

tea cup tightly, raising up to her mouth, gulping and got up, leaving me with her unfinished pizza slice. In my mind, I tried not to be sidetracked by my own views.

8. THE JUICE OF THE TRUTH

I noticed my mom was a bit gloomy, even though outwardly she was showing happiness on her face. Today, for the first time in her life she got up later than me : 6 am. I was leaving for my yoga class, and gently knocked on her door. She got up with a start, and realizing the time rushed to the washroom. I bade her good morning and left the house. All the other students of yoga had assembled and Bharati had already started her session. She welcome me with a nod and continued deep breathing exercises— the starting point of Yoga regime.

I realized I could not concentrate on the exercises as my mind was full of concern for mom. What happened? She was always cheerful and never complained. I suppressed my thoughts and tried to concentrate on yogic exercises. Bending down and touching my feet was more comfortable and I could see Bharati craning her neck to see all the sixteen students were doing correct poses. Turn by turn, she asked a volunteer to come and take her place for the next exercise, seeing the individual progress of each one of us. She was a dedicated YOGA Teacher and we appreciated her dedicated attention to all of us.

With yoga session over, I rushed down to my apartment to see the condition of my mom. She was cool and preparing a breakfast for me. I asked mom what was bothering her, and why she looked a little sad. "Nothing" she replied and served me a sandwich and a cup of *kadak* chai. "Ok, sonny, go to office with Happy Thoughts, and don't worry about me, I am perfectly OK, just it happens sometimes. I was relieved with her statement but an undercurrent told me she was lying. Not wishing to upset her, I quickly dressed up, though early, to go to the office. At least, a little separation will ease both of us, I felt. As I stepped outside the door, Angela called me "Good morning, hope all OK with you, was wondering why you did not call me in the last few days." I replied all is well and I shall meet you on the weekend at "SendUSLikes," *if you like* I stressed the words ! There was a little giggle from her and the conversation ended. I gathered speed, wishing to be more early in the office and clear office work. During this last week, we have quarter ending closing to do and I better be more attentive. I would certainly engage Krishna and if God wishes, I could also be training a new hand in the nick of time. I suddenly remembered Raj Sikander. Yes, I had met the man, but really not gone through his CV— had just passed to Krishna, who had okayed the candidate, giving him AAA rating. Yes, let me go to office and the first thing I will do, is get hold of his CV from Sheela's desk and concentrate on it.

There was an abrupt announcement from the Metro station informing the south bound Metro will be running 15 minutes late. "Oh ! Oh !, here I was thinking to reach earlier to office and there was a delay in Metro schedule ! What a pity! However, since I was much earlier than usual, I did not see much of a time loss. In the unforgiven time loss, I saw the face of my mom crying. "What was happening to me? I pinched my forearm to wake up and concentrated on the day's inning. The Metro just announced the arrival of train to Jabal Ali and I was caught up in the rush to alight the train pushing aside all thoughts. Good riddance. Even the morning call of Angela, I had not liked. However, the moving train moved my thoughts back to the office and I felt much better. The sight of a few moving abras along the creek, observed from a moving train, enlightened my mind. I smiled to myself unknowingly.

Back in the office, Ramu informed me, Sheela had just phoned reporting sick. I was taken back a little, feeling the displeasure she had shown at Harilal's comments yesterday. However, without prejudice, I went to Sheela's seat and picked up Raj Sikander's CV.

It was a three-page long CV neatly drafted, with his photo attached and his signature, neatly signed, running across his photo. I went minutely through his CV and read his employment history. He had changed only 2 jobs in his career of 7 years — the last one was with MARGOA ENTERPRISES FZE – only 4 months worked with them!

Suddenly my eyes popped out, and once again I read the company name: MARGOA ENTERPRISES FZE.

I called my boss, Harilal, deliberately, for my own specific reasons. He picked up the call noticing my early call time and cell number. "I need a favor from you, Sir" The candidate Raj is the best performer among the rest of the candidates, also he is out of job now, needs employment, has not quoted any starting salary needed. Krishna Pillai gave him a reasonable Test Paper, which he did alright.

On my part, I can commit you my support for training and assistance to Raj, for a period of two weeks, after office hours, or on holidays too. The very fact Sheela's brother knows him is also an advantage – a known devil is better ….. Harilal cut me short and asked "How much salary he is expecting? I replied "being known to Sheela he must be knowing we are not paymasters, yet he has approached us, we should consider him, as I too won't be very long with you. Harilal understood and asked me to call Raj today at eleven o'clock for an interview with him.

Highly pleased with my first round of efforts, I prayed to God to let Raj join us as soon as possible. I too could discreetly come to know about his resignation from …..

My cell phone rang, I first hesitated to pick up the call, then on second thoughts, since it was a local number, I picked up. A pleasant voice answered, "Good morning, am I talking to Robin?""Yes, you are, and who is this?" I politely asked. "I am Raj Sikander, and I want to thank you for the time and patience your office gave me while conducting the interview. I have already got an employment and shall not be available to join you…. Have A Good Day", and the line got disconnected. For a moment I was stunned. The cell phone dropped from my hand and somehow, I sank into my chair. Ramu came running to me "Sir, you OK? "Just leave me alone" and made a sign for him to go away.

It was not that we could not get any other capable candidate, but the shock of learning that Raj Sikander had resigned from Margoa Enterprises FZE, in four months' time! What could be the reason? Margoa was a paymaster, surely he must be drawing double of what our company was going to pay him. Would I tail Sheela and try to meet

Raj and find out the reasons for his resignation? Certainly No, in that case, my future employment would become known to Sheela and our office world. I did not want to happen this as my present situation was very precarious. My heart kept a foot away from the name of Margoa….. This was a bad omen and my ribs shook. Certainly, I would discuss this case with my mom and also get advice from Bharati, apart from Angela.

The rest of the day was uneventful, and no candidates came for any interview, even if they had come, I would have sent to Krishna. Sulking, I left homewards.

9. THE LAW OF THE LAND

We try to do good in life, yet, at some point in time, you feel you do not get justice. If others too feel the same, then who is right? Perplexing question, yet this was the reality, my mind replied. You are too alone in the world to understand everything. Yes, I recalled now, why was my mom feeling so grumpy in the morning? Did she have a premotion of something unpleasant going to happen. My joy of getting a new job was sandwiched between "go ahead" and "don't go ahead "dilemma. Yet, I trusted my mom and Bharati and would certainly get a refined thought from them. That was the Law of the Hand and not of land!

Mom had already prepared a nice cup of tea, and I could get the fragrance from just outside the door. I rushed to the washroom, changed clothes, and settled myself for the cup of tea, hoping it was not cold. Sipping a little tea, I relaxed and told my mom everything about Raj, and how I was feeling so depressed — confused with my own thoughts— to join Margoa.... or ignore the opportunity. My mom took a deep breath and replied "why are you so worried on that angle : you don't know his cause of resignation, and you should neither worry about it. Go ahead, as you have already tendered your resignation, got the go ahead from Chandulal or whoever …why do you want to look back? I would even go one more step: don't dig Sheela for any answer. What for? Trust yourself more than anyone else. Remember, over thinking is the biggest cause of our unhappiness. Keep your mind off such things, which don't help you anyway.

What astounding replies my mom gave! I was thrilled. This is what I like about moms—they know many things you even don't have an inkling about. A voice from inside me brought an unknown quote: God couldn't be everywhere, so HE made mothers ! How true, I murmured to myself. The water was in my house and I was going to the well….

There was another thought worrying me and I asked my mom: You appeared sulky, got up late in the morning: Is all OK with you mom? Did you have lunch today? Mom, assured me, all is fine: with sobbing voice, I cried "you are my world, please tell me truth. Suddenly she turned pale, a bit upset, I felt. "Yes, there is something and I shall tell you tonight. First you go and meet Angela, she called me in the afternoon, just checking on me. She is a real darling. Go and meet her. "No, mom, no… if you have something to tell me, tell me now, Angela can wait. "Do as I suggest as, in the meantime I will go for a walk and meet Bharati in the park. Bharati had called me in the afternoon, and I gave her my word. "No, mom this will not work for me: I won't feel comfortable till I know your cause of worry" I replied wearily. "Okay" she said : "Listen, I wanted to tell you yesterday, when it was your dads' – D anniversary. It was twenty-eight years ago. Your dad, although loving and caring, was an absolute alcoholic. One day, he had too much, and was driving his motorcycle rashly and banged into a stationary trailer, got badly hit, and was hospitalized for several weeks. You were two years old at that time. Each passing day, he was getting more hurt and angrier with himself. He realized it was his big mistake and could not forgive himself. Next morning the nurse found him motionless. There were tears in my mother's eyes, and mine too; and this was the secret she told me: – The Gift Of Anger buried in her heart for twenty eight years, and now you know.

To smoothen our nerves, I decided it was fair for both of us to part for a while and then meet. I dialed Angela's number, there was no answer. Yet, I went to "SendMeLikes" café knowing, by the time I reach there, she will call me. It was just twenty minutes away, but sometimes, St. Mary's Road is busy, and you must dodge through the crowd to make your way towards the café. Upon reaching, I called Angela again, and she answered: on my way to Café, walking from the church road. We just ordered tea and samosas. I told Angela my day's innings. She simply laughed and made no comments but wished me good luck for the new venture and left hurriedly saying her mom was unwell, and she needed to go. She took a few hasty steps and was soon out of sight through the evening crowd. Even my mind was uneasy. Back home, mom had just finished her porridge and said she was okay with a light meal. She asked me about Angela, and I said she was fine, and we met only for a few minutes as she had to rush back home as her mother was not keeping well.

10. A Taste of Freedom

My eye was on MERRY PLAZA since alighting from the Metro. I remembered the office was 206 and stood in line for the elevator to come. Finally, when the lift door opened, I crept in narrowly as there was hardly any space. A lot of people came out of the lift on the second floor. As I went towards office 206, I noticed 2 other people also crept into office 206 and they greeted "Good Morning" to Rosy Roshan. So did I. Rosy told me to take a seat and would attend to me in 2 minutes. Meanwhile, the two gentlemen who had entered with me disappeared in the corridor alongside the reception area.

Rosy was busy on the intercom. A man came from the corridor and gave the envelope to Rosy. Rosy called me to follow her and took me to the meeting room, carefully giving me the envelope and asking me to read: It was a Welcome letter addressed to me and informing me of my post, office timings, the departments, and the names of departmental heads. At the bottom of the letter, names of our associate offices with location, addresses and contact details were written. Below this information was a nice catchy sentence, written in bold print: **Giving Gets**

You: perhaps, the motto of the company. I was visibly impressed and very pleased with this kind of welcome letter. Surely, Henry Phil was a distinguished employer.

Next, Rosy told me she would introduce me to the rest of the office staff and called out to Santosh Pillai, the company PRO, to show me my seat, while she disappeared in the front office. Pillai called me to follow him and led me to the room upstairs. I could hear voices and saw the two gentlemen whom I had seen in the lift. "Your seat is at the far end. The seat on your left is occupied by Tim Sanders, and on the right is my seat. The next room is our sales department. Now, I am going down, in case you need anything, connect by inter com with Rosy. As soon as he left, Rosy entered the room, and called Tim Sanders and introduced me:" Meet Tim Sanders, Senior Accountant, 'Mr. Sanders, this is Mr Robin Marks, our new chief Accountant" "Good Morning Tim Sanders", I replied. He nodded replying: "Welcome Robin Marks, pleased to meet you" and silently moved away to his seat. Rosy looked at me and said "I suppose you have met Santosh Pillai the guy who escorted you here, our PRO. In the afternoon, there is a Sales meeting, and I shall introduce our sales team later: Catherine Toledo, Tony Miranda, Joe Philips, and Lobo Fernandes, who are now in the field. So, saying she went to the stairs, turning behind, she said "Phil will be arriving any moment now, and I shall inform him you have reported, and she went down by the staircase, nudging Tim in a friendly way. Tim came towards me and handed me a folder saying you can go through it: it is our company profile. Later you can log on to the laptop and get a password from Rosy. Maybe she has sent you an email by now. Please check. I checked my WhatsApp and noticed she had just sent me a password for me: ROBI0490 and requested acknowledgement of this email. I did so. In my mind I said this office is so organized and systematic.

We heard soft steps of someone coming up the stairs. Joe called out, our boss had arrived, and all went back to their respective seats. After a few moments, Rosy came up and informed all staff to join for a meeting room in Phil's room."Hello, Robin Marks, Welcome on Board"giving a little clap, others following him by clapping simultaneously. Rosy took a position in command and informed she had already introduced Robin to all colleagues and given him the "Welcome Letter". Tim had also given the Company Profile to Robin. "Well done, Rosy. Phil continued "And now "pointing to me, "Robin, tell us briefly about yourself to acquaint us about you. I was honored and could not believe such a reception !

I spoke briefly about my career graph and educational certificates achieved, ending with a "Thank You All" for a hearty welcome, and hope to continue with you for a long time.

Phil raised his hand and we all looked at him "Mark, You said you hope to continue with us for a long time" …..Yes, Rosy has been with us since the inception of my company, Tim Sanders is now 25 years with us, Pillai has been with us for over twenty years now, Lobo too is an old timer "Lobo, how many years you have been with us, tell us " "60 years" Lobo bluntly replied…. Phil laughed, that must be your age…. And we realized Lobo had joked about the length of service, and we all laughed Sir, I am 5 feet, two inches, Joe chipped in, creating more laughter …... Phil raised his hand, cutting through the laughter …..

Okay, Cheers to all, let us get back to our jobs. "Mark, you go through the Profile of our company, and log on to your laptop, go briefly through our accounts and familiarize yourself with the accounts. Just one more thing, Phil called Rosy and asked: where is the sitting arrangement of Robin? Rosy replied – the same chair where Raj Sikander was sitting. There was a pause and momentarily Robin felt unnerved. "No, move his chair towards my room, there is more space on that side, I feel." saying that Phil left. For no reason, Lobo raised his thumbs up.

"Rosy, confirm my business visit to Tokyo, next Monday for a period of three days, but before that send email to Taiki Tagashi to reconfirm his availability. For now, ask Catherine to organize a Sales meeting at 2pm today. Include Robin too.

We all dispersed to our respective seats. I got engrossed with the work on hand. There was a buzz on my intercom for the Sales meeting being conducted by Sales Manager, Catherine Toledo. In the meeting room, Catherine had ear marked on the board: Topic "Sales and Collections Targeted and Achieved. Please bring your previous notes of last meeting conducted, and hand a copy of the same to our New Chief Accountant, Robin Marks.

The sales meeting started at 2pm and ended around 4.30pm. I was told to keep track of the minutes and circulate the minutes at the end of the meeting, which I did. Phil left about 10 minutes prior to the end of the meeting, reminding me to send him the minutes of the meeting, once completed.

It was my first day at the office and I guessed I had a lot to talk about it to my mom.

She deserved a big break like me. It was her long-dedicated prayers and good wishes that netted this fortune. Now I realized she was praying for me the other day, while I thought she was a bit let down. **Yes, Giving is Getting, she got me what I was not getting.**

Angela and my mom were already seated on the sofa when I reached home. Angela whispered "Here comes **Good News** "And I have a token of a **Tea-CUP** that **Cheers…And Hello. You, OK?** She smiled, looking at my **MOM.**

Preface: The Gift of Anger

Robin, a charismatic young man is leading a simple life with his mother. Desiring a change in his work life, he goes for an interview, is successful, but hesitates to join as he is working in a comfort zone. He realizes the worldly ways when his boss acts tough and throws an axe in his plans. Determined to succeed, he devises a plan to overcome the situation which fails him at the last moment. He is at sixes and seven when he re-engineers his plans and is saved by a shadow behind him. A gripping tale of lone wolf in the maze of life.

www.ingramcontent.com/pod-product-compliance
Lightning Source LLC
Chambersburg PA
CBHW031329130726
47988CB00007B/3049